RAINBOW
magic®

To the fairies at the
bottom of my garden

Special thanks to
Narinder Dhami

ORCHARD BOOKS
338 Euston Road, London NW1 3BH
Orchard Books Australia
Level 17/207 Kent Street, Sydney, NSW 2000
A Paperback Original

First published in 2003 by Orchard Books.

© 2008 Rainbow Magic Limited.
A HIT Entertainment company. Rainbow Magic
is a trademark of Rainbow Magic Limited.
Reg. U.S. Pat. & Tm. Off. And other countries.
www.rainbowmagiconline.com

Illustrations © Georgie Ripper 2003

A CIP catalogue record for this book is available
from the British Library.

ISBN 978 1 84362 019 8
42

Printed in Great Britain

Orchard Books is a division of Hachette Children's Books,
an Hachette Livre UK company

www.hachettelivre.co.uk

Fern
the Green
Fairy

by Daisy Meadows

illustrated by Georgie Ripper

ORCHARD

Jack Frost's Ice Castle

Tom Goodfellow's House

Merry-go-round

Mrs Merry's Cottage

Willow Tree

Stream

Field

Town

Mermaid Cottage

Harbour

Dolphin Cottage

Cold winds blow and thick ice form,
I conjure up this fairy storm.
To seven corners of the mortal world
the Rainbow Fairies will be hurled!

I curse every part of Fairyland,
with a frosty wave of my icy hand.
For now and always, from this fateful day,
Fairyland will be cold and grey!

Ruby, Amber and Saffron
are out of danger.
Will Rachel and Kirsty free
Fern the **Green Fairy** too?

Contents

The Secret Garden

"Oh!" Rachel Walker gasped in delight, as she gazed around her. "What a perfect place for a picnic!"

"It's a secret garden," Kirsty Tate said, her eyes shining.

They were standing in a large garden. It looked as if nobody else had been there for a long, long time.

Pink and white roses grew all around
the tree trunks, filling the air with sweet
perfume. White marble statues stood
here and there, half hidden by trailing,
green ivy. And right in the middle of
the garden was a crumbling stone
tower.

"There was a castle here once called
Moonspinner Castle," Mr Walker said,
looking at his guidebook. "But now all
that's left is the tower."

Rachel and Kirsty stared up at the ruined tower. The yellow stones glowed warmly in the sunshine. They were covered in soft, green moss. Near the top of the tower was a small, square window.

"It's just like Rapunzel's tower," Kirsty said. "I wonder if we can get up to the top?"

"Let's go and see!" Rachel said eagerly. "I want to explore the whole garden. Can we, Mum?"

"Off you go," smiled Mrs Walker. "Your dad and I will get the food ready." She opened the picnic basket. "But don't be too long, girls."

Rachel and Kirsty rushed over to the door in the side of the tower. Kirsty tugged at the heavy iron handle. But the door was locked.

Rachel felt disappointed. "Oh, that's a shame," she said.

Kirsty sighed. "Yes, I was hoping Fern the Green Fairy might be here."

Rachel and Kirsty had a secret. They were helping to find the seven Rainbow Fairies before the end of their holiday on Rainspell Island. The fairies had been cast out of Fairyland by evil Jack Frost, and Fairyland had lost all its colour. Only when all seven fairies returned home would Fairyland be bright and beautiful again.

"Fern," Rachel called in a low voice. "Are you here?"

Here... Here... Here...
Her words echoed off the stones. Rachel and Kirsty held their breath and waited. But they couldn't hear anything except leaves rustling in the breeze.

"It's such a special place," Kirsty said. "It *feels* like there's magic close by." Then she gasped and pointed. "Rachel, look at the ivy!"

Rachel stared. Glossy green leaves grew thickly on the wall, but in one place the stones were bare, in the shape of a perfect circle.

Rachel's heart began to beat faster.
"It's just like a fairy ring!" she said. She
ran round the tower to take a closer
look, and almost tripped over the lace of
one of her trainers.

"Careful!" Kirsty said,
grabbing Rachel's arm.

Rachel sat down
on a mossy stone to
retie her shoelace.
"There's green
everywhere ," she
said, looking round
at the lush grass and
the leafy trees. "Fern
must be here."

"We'd better find her quickly then,"
Kirsty said with a shiver. "In case Jack
Frost's goblins find her first!"

Jack Frost had sent his goblin servants to Rainspell. He wanted them to stop the fairies from getting home to Fairyland.

"Where shall we start looking?" Rachel asked, standing up again.

Kirsty laughed. "You've got green stuff all over you!" she said.

Rachel twisted round to look. The back of her denim skirt was green and dusty. "It must be the moss," she grumbled, brushing it off.

The dust flew up into the air. It sparkled and glittered in the morning sun. As it fell to the ground, tiny, green leaves appeared and the smell of freshly cut grass filled the air.

Rachel and Kirsty turned to each other. "It's fairy dust!" they gasped together.

Where is Fern?

"Fern *is* here!" said Kirsty.

"Thank goodness I sat down on that fairy dust!" Rachel said.

They walked all round the tower, looking under bushes and inside sweet-smelling flowers. As they walked, they softly called Fern's name. But the Green Fairy was nowhere to be found.

19

"You don't think the goblins have caught her, do you?" Rachel said, feeling very worried.

"I hope not," replied Kirsty. "I'm sure Fern *was* here, but now she's somewhere else."

"Yes, but where?" Rachel looked round the garden in despair.

"Maybe there's magic around to help us," Kirsty said hopefully.

She looked down at the tiny leaves. Some of them had begun to flutter across the garden. "I know, let's follow the fairy dust."

The bright green leaves floated over to a narrow path that led into a beautiful orchard. Rachel could see apples, pears and plums growing on the trees.

"It's a magic trail!" Kirsty breathed.

"Quick, let's keep following the fairy dust," Rachel said.

Rachel and Kirsty set off along the path, which twisted and turned through the fruit trees.

Suddenly the path opened out into a
large clearing. Kirsty's eyes opened
wide when she saw what was in front
of them. "It's a maze!" she cried.

The thick, green hedges loomed
above them, their leaves rustling softly.

Rachel nudged Kirsty. "Look," she
pointed. "The fairy trail goes right into
the maze!"

"We'll have to follow it," Kirsty said bravely.

The two girls followed the floating fairy leaves through the narrow entrance. Kirsty felt a bit scared as the fairy dust led them first one way, then another between the green hedges. What if the trail ran out and they got lost in the maze?

"Maybe there'll be another clue in the middle of the maze," Rachel said hopefully.

"Or maybe Fern will be there!" Kirsty added.

They turned one more corner and suddenly the hedges parted to reveal the centre of the maze. A nut tree stood in the very middle. The fairy dust led right to the bottom of the tree, then stopped. "Fern must be here!" Rachel said excitedly.

Kirsty frowned. "Yes, but *where*?" she asked, looking round.

Tap! Tap! Tap!
The two girls jumped.
"What was that?" Rachel gasped.

There it was again. *Tap! Tap! Tap!*
Kirsty's eyes opened wide. "It's coming from over there." She pointed at the nut tree.

"I hope it isn't a goblin trap," Rachel whispered.

Tap! Tap! Tap!

The noise was louder now. Slowly Rachel and Kirsty walked right round the tree. At first they couldn't see anything unusual.

Then Rachel pointed at the trunk. "What's a *window* doing in a *tree*?" she gasped.

There was a small, hollow knot halfway up the trunk – and it was covered by a glass window!

Kirsty put out her hand and touched the window. It was very cold and wet. "It's not glass," she whispered. "It's *ice*!"

Both girls looked more closely.
Suddenly, something moved behind the
icy window. Kirsty could just make out
a tiny girl dressed in glittering green.

"Rachel, we've found her!" she said
happily. "It's Fern, the Green Fairy!"

Lost in the Maze

Fern waved to the girls through the sheet of ice. Her mouth opened and closed, but Rachel and Kirsty couldn't hear a word she was saying. The ice was too thick.

Rachel looked worried. "She must be freezing in there," she said. "We've got to get her out."

"We could smash the ice with a stick," said Kirsty. Then she frowned. "But Fern might get hurt."

Rachel thought hard. "We could *melt* the ice," she said.

"How?" Kirsty asked.

"Like this," Rachel replied. She reached up and pressed her hand firmly against the window of ice. Kirsty did the same. The ice felt freezing cold, but they kept on pressing against it with their warm hands.

Soon, a few drops of water began to trickle down the window.

"It's melting!" Rachel said. "We can make a hole in it now." She gently poked the middle of the window with her finger, and the ice began to crack.

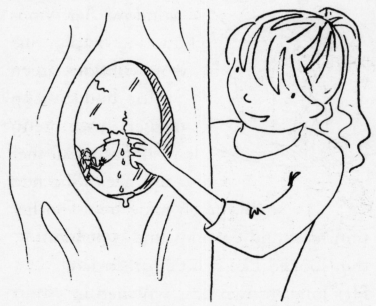

"Don't worry, Fern," cried Kirsty. "You'll be out of there very soon!"

There was a sudden crack, as the ice
split open. A flash of sparkling fairy
dust shot out, leaving behind a lovely
scent of cut grass. And then Fern
the Green Fairy pushed her
way out of the icy
window, her wings
fluttering limply. She
wore a bright green
top and stretchy
trousers, with pretty
leaf shapes round her
waist and neck. She had
small, green pixie boots on her
tiny feet, and earrings and a pendant
that looked like a little, green leaf.
Her long, brown hair was tied in
bunches, and her slender, emerald
wand was tipped with gold.

"Oh, I'm s-s-so c-c-cold!" the fairy
gasped, shivering all over. She floated
down to rest on Kirsty's shoulder.

"Let me warm you up a bit," said
Rachel. She scooped the fairy up and
held her in her cupped hands. Then she
blew gently on her.

The warmth of Rachel's breath
seemed to do the trick. Fern stopped
shivering, and her wings straightened
out. "Thank you," she said. "I feel
much better now."

"I'm Rachel and this is Kirsty,"
Rachel explained. "We're here to take
you to the pot-at-the-end-
of-the-rainbow."

"Ruby, Amber
and Saffron
are waiting
for you,"
Kirsty added.
Fern's green
eyes lit up.
"They're safe!"
she exclaimed.
"That's wonderful!"
She flew off Rachel's
hand in a blaze of green
fairy dust and twirled joyfully
in the air. "But what about my other
sisters?"

"Don't worry, we're going to find them too," Kirsty told her. "How did you get stuck behind the ice window?"

"When I landed on Rainspell Island, I got tangled up in the ivy on the tower," Fern explained. "I managed to untangle myself, but then Jack Frost's goblins started chasing me. So I ran into the maze and hid in the nut tree. But it was raining, and when the goblins passed by, the rainwater turned to ice. So I was trapped."

Suddenly Rachel shivered. "It's getting colder," she said. She glanced up at the sky. The sun had disappeared behind a cloud, and there was a sudden chill in the air.

"The goblins must be close by!" Kirsty gasped, looking scared.

Fern nodded. "Yes, we'd better get out of this garden right away," she said calmly. "You know the way, don't you?"

Rachel and Kirsty looked at each other.

"I'm not sure," Kirsty said with a frown. "Do *you* know, Rachel?"

Rachel shook her head. "No," she replied. "But we can follow the fairy trail back to the start of the maze."

Kirsty looked around. "Where *is* the fairy trail?" she asked.

An icy breeze was blowing all around them now. The green fairy leaves were drifting away and vanishing in front of their very eyes.

"Oh no!" Kirsty gasped. "What are we going to do now?"

Suddenly they heard the sound of heavy footsteps coming through the maze towards them.

"I know that fairy is in here *somewhere*," grumbled a loud, gruff voice.

Fern, Rachel and Kirsty stared at each other in dismay.

"Goblins!" whispered Rachel.

Fairy Fireworks

Rachel, Kirsty and Fern listened in horror as the goblins came closer. As usual, they were arguing with each other.

"Come on!" snorted one goblin. "We can't let her get away again."

"Stop bossing me about," whined the other one. "I'm going as fast as I can. OW!"

There was a loud *THUD!* It sounded as if the goblin had fallen over.

"If your feet weren't so big, you wouldn't trip over them," jeered the first goblin.

"They're big enough to give you a good kick!" the other goblin snapped.

"Let's hide in the tree," Fern whispered to Rachel and Kirsty. "I'll make you fairy-sized, so we can all fit under a leaf." Quickly she shot up into the air and sprinkled the girls with fairy dust. Rachel and Kirsty gasped as they felt themselves shrinking, down and down.

It was so exciting!

Fern took the girls' hands. "Let's go," she said, and the three of them fluttered up into the air and landed on a branch.

Fat brown hazelnuts grew on the tree, as big as beachballs. Even the thinnest twigs looked like tree trunks to the tiny girls! Fern heaved up the edge of a leaf, which was as big as a tablecloth, and they all crept underneath.

A moment later, the goblins rushed into the clearing.

"Where can that fairy be?" grumbled one of them. "I know she came this way!"

They began to search around the bottom of the tree.

"How are we going to get back to the pot?" Rachel whispered to Fern.

Fern laughed. "Don't worry! I think I know someone who can help us!" And she pointed past them.

Rachel and Kirsty turned to look.
A furry, grey face was peeping shyly
round the tree trunk. It was a squirrel.

"Hello," Fern called softly.

The squirrel jumped and hid behind
the trunk. Then he peeped out again,
his dark eyes curious.

"Maybe he'd like a hazelnut?"
Kirsty suggested.

There was a big, shiny nut growing
right next to her. She
wrapped her arms around
it, but she couldn't pull
it off the twig. Rachel
and Fern came to
help. All three of
them tugged at the
nut until it came off
the branch with a jump.

43

Fern held it out to the squirrel.
"Mmm, a yummy nut!" she said.

The squirrel ran lightly along the
branch, his long, furry tail waving. He
took the hazelnut and held it in his
front paws.

"What's your name?" asked Fern
kindly.

"I'm Fluffy," squeaked the squirrel,
between nibbles.

"I'm Fern," said the fairy. "And these are my friends, Rachel and Kirsty. We need to get away from the goblins. Will you help us?"

Fluffy shivered. "I don't like goblins," he squeaked.

"We won't let them hurt you," Fern promised, stroking his head. "Can you give us a ride on your back? You can jump from hedge to hedge much better than we can! We have to get out of the maze."

"Yes, I'll help you," Fluffy agreed, finishing the last piece of nut.

Rachel, Kirsty and Fern climbed on to the squirrel's back. Kirsty thought it was just like sinking into a big, soft blanket.

"This is lovely," said Fern, snuggling down into the squirrel's fur. "Let's go, Fluffy!"

The squirrel turned and ran along the branch. Rachel, Kirsty and Fern clung tightly to Fluffy's thick fur as he jumped out of the tree, right over the goblins' heads! He landed neatly on the nearest hedge. The goblins were so busy arguing, they didn't even notice.

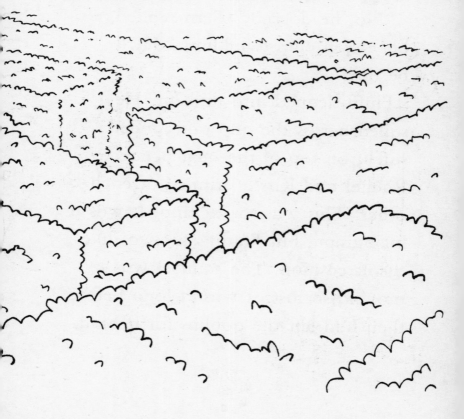

Fern leaned forward to whisper in
the squirrel's ear. "Well done,
Fluffy. Now the next one!"

Rachel gulped when she saw
how far away the next hedge was.
"Maybe Fluffy needs some fairy
magic to help him," she said.

"No, he doesn't," Fern replied,
her green eyes twinkling. "He'll
be fine!"

Fluffy leaped into mid-air. He
sailed across the gap and landed
safely on top of the next hedge.
Rachel and Kirsty grinned at each
other. This was so exciting! It was a
bit bumpy, but Fluffy's fur was like
a soft cushion. The squirrel was
moving so fast, it wasn't long before
they had left the goblins far behind.

"Here we are," Fern said at last, as Fluffy reached the edge of the maze. "Now which way do we go, girls?"

Rachel and Kirsty looked at each other in dismay. "This isn't the way we came *in*," Rachel said. "And I don't know the way back to the pot. Do you, Kirsty?"

Kirsty shook her head.

Fern looked worried. "But I have to get back to the pot!" she said.

"Oh!" Kirsty had an idea. "Rachel, what about looking in our magic bags?"

"Good idea," Rachel agreed.

Titania, the Fairy Queen, had given Rachel and Kirsty two special magic bags, for whenever they needed help. The girls took the bags with them everywhere.

Fluffy scrambled down the hedge to the ground, and Rachel, Kirsty and Fern climbed off his back. Kirsty opened her rucksack and looked inside. One of the magic bags was glowing with a silvery light. "I wonder what's inside?" she said, reaching in.

She pulled out a thin, green tube, covered with sparkling gold stars.

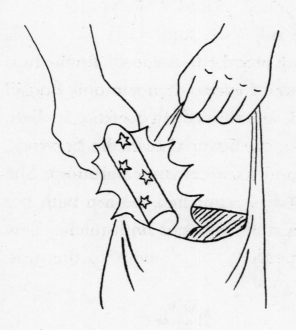

"It looks like a *firework*," Rachel said. "That's not much use, is it?"

"It's a fairy firework!" said Fern excitedly. "We can shoot it into the sky, and my sisters will see it from the pot. Then they'll know we need help."

"But what about the goblins?" Rachel asked. "Won't they see it too, and know where we are?"

Fern looked serious. "We've got to take the risk," she said.

Kirsty stood the firework firmly in a patch of earth, then she and Rachel moved away from it. Fern hovered over the firework, her wings fluttering. She touched the top with her wand and quickly flew back to the girls.

Rachel and Kirsty held their breath as the tube caught light. Suddenly, with a loud fizz the whole firework shot upwards, trailing bright green sparks behind it. It climbed higher and higher into the sky, until it burst in a shower of emerald stars. The stars spelt out the words

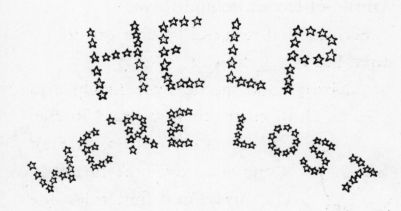

HELP WE'RE LOST

They twinkled brightly in the darkening sky before fading away.

"We won't have to wait long," Fern said. "Help will come very soon."

Rachel and Kirsty wondered what was going to happen. How could the fairies come to their rescue? They weren't supposed to leave the clearing where the pot was, in case the goblins found them. Suddenly, there was a rustle of leaves behind them.

"Did you see that fairy firework?" shouted a loud voice. "It came from over there. Quick, before that fairy gets away again!"

Hedgehog Help

Rachel and Kirsty stared at each other
in alarm. Fluffy looked scared too. The
goblins were on their trail again!

"They're coming towards us,"
Rachel whispered as the voices got
louder.

"Don't worry," Fern said, smiling.
"My sisters will send help quickly."

Then Rachel spotted a line of golden sparkles twinkling towards them through the fruit trees. "What's that?" she whispered.

"Is it goblin magic?" Kirsty asked anxiously.

Fern shook her head. "They're fireflies! My sisters must have sent them to show us the way back to the pot."

Suddenly there was another shout from inside the maze. "Look, what are those lights over there?"

"The goblins have spotted the fireflies!" Rachel gasped.

"Quickly, Fluffy!" Fern said, as they climbed on to the squirrel's back again. "Follow the fireflies!"

The golden specks were dancing away through the trees. Fluffy scampered after them, just as the goblins dashed out of the maze.

"There's the fairy!" one of them shouted, pointing at Fern. "Stop that squirrel!"

"Come back!" the other roared as Fluffy ran off.

Rachel, Kirsty and Fern clung
to Fluffy's fur as the
squirrel zig-zagged
this way and that
to get away from
the goblins. Fluffy
scrambled up the
trunk of the nearest
tree. He was just
about to jump across
to the next, when someone
called to them from below.

"Hello!"

"Who's that?" Rachel asked.
She, Kirsty and Fern peered
down at the ground.
A hedgehog was
standing at the foot
of the apple tree.

"Hello," he called again. "The animals in the garden have heard that you're in trouble. We'd like to help."

"Oh, thank you," Fern called. Then she gasped as the two goblins appeared among the trees.

"Where's that squirrel gone?" one of them yelled.

Quickly Fluffy leaped across to the next apple tree. The goblins roared with rage and dashed forward. At that very moment, the hedgehog curled himself into a ball and rolled right into their path. Rachel thought he looked like a big, prickly football.

"OW!" both goblins howled. "My toes!"

Rachel and Kirsty couldn't help laughing as the goblins jumped around holding their feet. "Hooray for Hedgehog!" they shouted.

As Fluffy jumped from one fruit tree to the next, the firefly lights behind them began to go out.

"Hey! Who turned off the lights?" wailed one of the goblins, still rubbing his foot. "Which way are we supposed to go?"

"How do I know, stupid?" snapped the other goblin. Their voices were getting fainter now as Fluffy hurried on.

"Thank you, fireflies," called Fern, waving at the last few specks of light. "Now we need to find a way to the orchard wall. We can't be far from the pot now."

"I can help you," a small voice whispered.

A fawn was standing at the bottom of the tree. Her golden brown coat was short and silky, and she stared up at them with big, brown eyes. "You mean you can show us the way?" Kirsty said. "Yes, I can," the deer nodded, twitching her little tail. "I can show you a short cut."

She trotted off through the trees on her long legs. Fluffy followed her, leaping from branch to branch above the little deer's head.

Rachel could hardly breathe for excitement. She was riding on a squirrel's back, being shown the way to the pot-at-the-end-of-the-rainbow by a fawn!

A few moments later they reached the brick wall which ran round the outside of the orchard. Fluffy leaped up to the top of the wall, and Rachel and Kirsty looked eagerly ahead of them. On the other side of the wall was a meadow, and beyond that a wood.

"Look!" Rachel shouted. "That's where the pot is!"

Flying High

"Thank you!" Kirsty and Rachel
called to the baby deer. She blinked
her long eyelashes at them, and
trotted away.

A blackbird with shiny, dark feathers
was sitting on the wall a little way
away. He hopped over to them, his
head on one side. "I'm here to take you

to the pot-at-the-end-of-the-rainbow,"
he chirped. "All aboard!"

Fluffy looked sad as Fern, Rachel and
Kirsty slid off his back and climbed on
to the blackbird. It was a tight squeeze,
and the feathers felt smooth and silky
after Fluffy's fur.

"Goodbye, Fluffy!" called Rachel,
and she blew him a kiss. She felt sad
to leave their new friend behind.

The blackbird soared into the air.

"Look for the big weeping willow tree," Rachel told the blackbird as he swooped across the meadow.

"I can't wait to see my sisters again," said Fern, sounding very excited.

The blackbird flew over the wood and landed in the clearing near the willow tree. Rachel, Kirsty and Fern jumped down on to the grass.

"Who's there?" croaked a stern voice. A plump, green frog hopped out from under the hanging branches of the tree.

"Bertram, it's me!" Fern called. Quickly the fairy waved her wand, and Rachel and Kirsty shot up to their normal size again. "Miss Fern!" Bertram said joyfully. "You're back!"

"We followed the fireflies," Fern said, giving the frog a hug. "Thank you for sending them."

"We saw the firework in the sky," Bertram explained, "so we knew you were in trouble. But you'll be safe here," he went on. "The pot is hidden under the tree."

Rachel and Kirsty hurried over and pulled aside the long branches. The pot-at-the-end-of-the-rainbow lay there on its side.

Suddenly a fountain of red, orange and yellow fairy dust whooshed out of the pot. Ruby, Amber and Saffron flew out, looking very excited. A big queen bee buzzed out behind them.

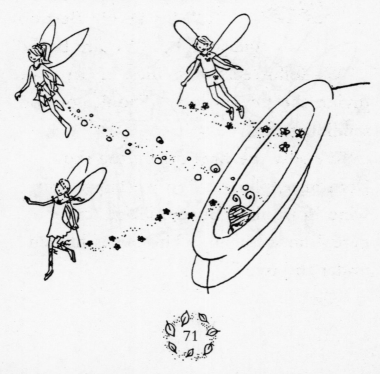

"Fern!" Ruby called. "You're safe! It's so good to see you!"

Rachel and Kirsty beamed as they watched the fairies hug each other. The air around them fizzed and popped with red flowers, green leaves, tiny, yellow butterflies and orange bubbles.

"We've really missed you," said
Saffron. Beside her, the bee nudged her
with a tiny feeler. "Oh, sorry,
Queenie," said Saffron. "This is my
sister, Fern."

Queenie buzzed, "Hello!"

"How did you get back so quickly?"
asked Amber. "We only sent the
fireflies a little while ago."

"Our woodland friends
helped us," Fern said. She
waved as the blackbird
flew off. "Especially Fluffy
the squirrel." She sighed. "It
was a shame we had to leave
him behind."

Ruby laughed. "Who's that then?" she
asked, pointing at a tree on the other
side of the clearing.

Rachel and Kirsty looked too. Fluffy was peeping at them from behind the tree trunk, looking very shy.

"Fluffy!" Fern flew over and hugged him. "What are you doing here?"

"I was worried about you," Fluffy explained shyly. "I wanted to make sure you got back to the pot safely."

"Would you like to stay with us too?" asked Amber. "You could live in the willow tree, couldn't you?"

"Yes, *please*," squeaked Fluffy.

Ruby turned to Rachel and Kirsty.

"Thank you again," she said. "I don't know what we'd do without you!"

Fern fluttered lightly on to Rachel's shoulder. One of her wings brushed softly against Rachel's cheek, like a butterfly. "We'll see you again soon, won't we?"

"Yes, of course," Rachel promised.

"Only three more Rainbow Fairies left to find!" Kirsty added. She took Rachel's hand and they waved to the fairies, before running out of the clearing. "We'd better get back to your mum and dad, Rachel. They'll be wondering where we are."

"Good idea," Rachel laughed. "We'd better hurry back, before my dad eats all the picnic!"

Now it's time for Kirsty and Rachel to help...

Sky the Blue Fairy

Read on for a sneak peek...

"The water's really warm!" laughed Rachel Walker. She was sitting on a rock, swishing her toes in one of Rainspell Island's deep, blue rock pools. Her friend Kirsty Tate was looking for shells on the rocks nearby.

"Mind you don't slip, Kirsty!" called Mrs Tate. She was sitting further down the beach with Mrs Walker.

"OK, Mum!" Kirsty yelled back. As she looked down at her bare feet, a patch of green seaweed began to move. There was something blue and shiny underneath it.

"Rachel! Come over here," she shouted.

Rachel went over to Kirsty. "What is it?" she asked.

Kirsty pointed to the seaweed. "There's something blue under there," she said. "I wonder, could it be…"

"Sky the Blue Fairy?" Rachel said eagerly.

Jack Frost had banished the seven Rainbow Fairies from Fairyland with a magic spell…

Read Sky the Blue Fairy to find out what adventures are in store for Kirsty and Rachel!

RAINBOW magic ®

Meet the fairies, play games
and get sneak peeks at
the latest books!

There's fairy fun for everyone at

www.rainbowmagicbooks.co.uk

You'll find great activities, competitions, stories and
fairy profiles, and also a special newsletter.

Win Rainbow Magic Goodies!

There are lots of Rainbow Magic fairies, and we want to know
which one is your favourite! Send us a picture of her and tell
us in thirty words why she is your favourite and why you like
Rainbow Magic books. Each month we will put the entries into
a draw and select one winner to receive a Rainbow Magic
Sparkly T-shirt and Goody Bag!

Send your entry on a postcard to Rainbow Magic Competition,
Orchard Books, 338 Euston Road, London NW1 3BH.
Australian readers should email: childrens.books@hachette.com.au
New Zealand readers should write to Rainbow Magic Competition,
PO Box 3255, Shortland St, Auckland 1140, NZ.
Don't forget to include your name and address.
Only one entry per child.

Good luck!

Meet the Weather Fairies

 Crystal the Snow Fairy

 Abigail the Breeze Fairy

 Pearl the Cloud Fairy

 Goldie the Sunshine Fairy

 Evie the Mist Fairy

 Storm the Lightning Fairy

 Hayley the Rain Fairy

Also available as an ebook

Join Rachel and Kirsty as they hunt for the
feathers that naughty Jack Frost has stolen
from Doodle the magic weather-vane cockerel!

www.rainbowmagicbooks.co.uk